HECTOR PROTECTOR
AND
AS I WENT OVER THE WATER

VICTOR

HECTOR PROTECTOR
AND
AS I WENT OVER THE WATER

TWO NURSERY RHYMES WITH PICTURES
BY
MAURICE SENDAK

HARPER & ROW · PUBLISHERS · NEW YORK

[redacted]

 • Library of Congress Catalog Card Number: 65–21388
Printed in the United States of America for Harper & Row, Publishers, Incorporated.
ISBN 0–06–025485–8 ISBN 0–06–025486–6 (lib. bdg.)

HECTOR PROTECTOR
FOR
SETH

Hector Protector was dressed all in green.

NO!
NO!

NO!
HO!

So!
NO NO NO!

I HATE GREEN!

Hector Protector was sent to the queen.

I HATE THE QUEEN!
CAKE
FOR HER HIGHNESS

GRR-R

GRR-R

SSS-S

QUEEN'S
ROOM

MOTHER GOOSE

The queen did not like him

no more did the king

BOW
WOW

so Hector Protector was sent back again.

BYE

OH!
CAKE
FOR HER HIGHNESS

NO!
HECTOR'S ROOM
HO!

NO!

NO!
FOR HER
HIGHNESS
CAKE

OH!

AS I WENT OVER THE WATER
FOR BARBARA

As I went over the water

VICTOR

the water went over me.

HEE HEE

I saw two little blackbirds sitting on a tree.

VICTOR

One called me a rascal

VICTOR

and one called me a thief.

VICTOR

I took up my little black stick

VICTOR

and knocked out all their teeth !

VICTOR

VICTOR

VICTOR

VICTOR